Hello, Family Members,

Learning to read is one of the most important accomplishments of early childhood. **Hello Reader!** books are designed to help children become skilled readers who like to read. Beginning readers learn to read by remembering frequently used words like "the," "is," and "and"; by using phonics skills to decode new words; and by interpreting picture and text clues. These books provide both the stories children enjoy and the structure they need to read fluently and independently. Here are suggestions for helping your child *before, during,* and *after* reading:

Before

- Look at the cover and pictures and have your child predict what the story is about.
- Read the story to your child.
- Encourage your child to chime in with familiar words and phrases.
- Echo read with your child by reading a line first and having your child read it after you do.

During

- Have your child think about a word he or she does not recognize right away. Provide hints such as "Let's see if we know the sounds" and "Have we read other words like this one?"
- Encourage your child to use phonics skills to sound out new words.
- Provide the word for your child when more assistance is needed so that he or she does not struggle and the experience of reading with you is a positive one.
- Encourage your child to have fun by reading with a lot of expression . . . like an actor!

After

- Have your child keep lists of interesting and favorite words.
- Encourage your child to read the books over and over again. Have him or her read to brothers, sisters, grandparents, and even teddy bears. Repeated readings develop confidence in young readers.
- Talk about the stories. Ask and answer questions. Share ideas about the funniest and most interesting characters and events in the stories.

I do hope that you and your child enjoy this book.

—Francie Alexander
Reading Specialist,
Scholastic's Learning Ventures

To Beth K., all my love

—L.B.

Go to scholastic.com for web site information on
Scholastic authors and illustrators.

ISBN 0-439-31706-1

Library of Congress Cataloging-in-Publication Data available

10 9 8 7 6 5   04 05
Printed in the U.S.A.   23
First printing, September 2001

by Kirsten Hall
Illustrated by Lindy Burnett

Hello Reader! — Level 3

SCHOLASTIC INC. Cartwheel B·O·O·K·S ®

New York   Toronto   London   Auckland   Sydney
Mexico City   New Delhi   Hong Kong

Today Mrs. Wong's class was going on its first trip of the year.

"A trip to a nature center sounds fun,"
Rika said, putting on her scarf.
"I can't wait to pet the rabbits."

"I hope we see some chipmunks,"
Amy said. "They're my favorite."

The class filed onto the school bus.
"Let's sit together," Rika said to Amy.
"How about over there?" Amy said.
She pointed to the back of the bus.

Daniel and Pedro sat down in the seat
behind the girls.
Rika and Amy groaned.
Last year Pedro had teased them during
the entire trip to the planetarium.

Mrs. Wong stood at the front of the bus.
"Class, I think you will enjoy the
nature center. Especially the bat cave!"

"Bat cave?" Rika said.

"I'm not so sure I want to go to the nature center now," Amy said.

"What if a vampire bat tries to bite me?"

"Vampire bat?" Daniel said.

He shivered. "Are there really vampire bats?"

Pedro laughed.

"Are you guys scared of flying mice?"
he asked.

"I've heard that bats are blind,"
Daniel said. "Is that true?"

"If it is, then one could fly right into
Amy's hair," Pedro said.

"Into my hair! Oh, no!" Amy said.
She pulled off her hat.
She dug in her pocket for a ponytail
holder and tied back her hair.

When the girls weren't looking,
Pedro leaned over their seat.
"I've come to suck your blood!"
he roared, just like Dracula.
Amy and Rika screamed.
Daniel ducked down in his seat and hid.

The bus pulled up to the nature center.
"We're here!" Mrs. Wong said.

"Class, this is Mr. Sullivan," Mrs. Wong said.
"He'll be showing us around the center.
He's a bat expert."

"Let's hold hands," Rika said to Amy.
"Then maybe we won't be scared."
"What babies!" said Pedro.

"Don't you ever get scared, Pedro?"
Amy asked.

"Me? Scared?" Pedro shook his head.
"I'm not afraid of anything. Especially
not bats."

The class walked into the bat cave.
From behind a glass window,
the kids could see bats everywhere.
Some were flying through the air.
Others were hanging upside down
from branches.
Amy and Rika stood close together.

Rika noticed a little bat all alone
on a branch.
"Look at this tiny one," she said.

Amy walked over to get a better look.

"He has a funny nose," Amy said.

"He's kind of cute," Rika said.

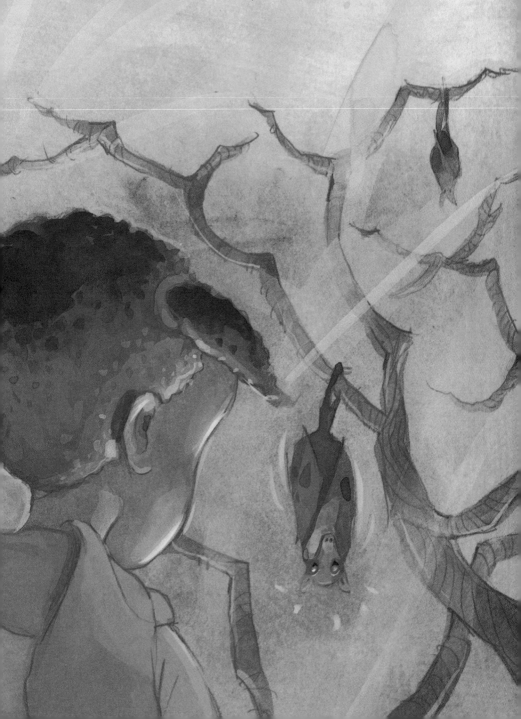

Rika looked for Pedro.
She wanted to tell him that she didn't see
any vampire bats.

Pedro was tying his shoelaces.
"Pedro!" Rika called out.

Pedro stood up.
A flying bat zoomed down from a
high branch.
It flapped its wings right near Pedro's face.
Then it flew away.
Pedro screamed and turned away.

"What's the matter, Pedro?"
Mrs. Wong said.
She ran over to him.
"That bat was coming after me!"
Pedro said. "He scared me!"

Mr. Sullivan walked over to Pedro.
"I bet that was scary," he said.
"But that bat was probably going after a bug.
And it's behind a glass window so it
wouldn't hurt you. In fact, bats help us
more than we know."

Mr. Sullivan turned to Mrs. Wong. "Maybe now would be a good time for the class to learn more about bats."

Mr. Sullivan told the class that bats aren't mice with wings.
He told them that bats are the only mammals that could fly.
He told them many more things about bats.

The class talked about some
of the things they learned.

On the bus ride back to school,
Pedro was quiet.
He sat by himself.
He didn't joke around or tease.

"What's the matter, Pedro?" Amy asked.

Pedro shrugged.

"Are you feeling okay?" Rika asked.

Pedro shrugged again.

Back at school, the class sat in a circle.
"What did you think of the bat cave?"
Mrs. Wong asked.
Rika raised her hand.
"It was neat! Bats aren't as scary
as I thought," she said.
"I never knew they did so many
good things."

"Tell us one good thing bats do,"
Mrs. Wong said.
"Bats eat mosquitoes," Rika said.
"And I'm glad they do.
I don't like mosquito bites!"
She made a funny face.

"Who else learned something interesting?" Mrs. Wong asked. Daniel raised his hand "Bats help lots of different fruits grow," he said, "like mangoes, peaches, and bananas."

Daniel smiled.
"That makes me like bats.
After all, without bats,
we wouldn't have banana splits!"
The class laughed again.

"Anyone else?" Mrs. Wong asked.
Amy raised her hand.

"Bats aren't blind.
Some bats can see with their eyes.
Other bats use radar."
Amy looked at Pedro.
"That means they don't fly into
people by mistake."

Pedro raised his hand.

"I learned something, too," he said.

"What was that?" Mrs. Wong asked.

"I learned not to make fun of my
friends when they're scared."

Mrs. Wong smiled.

"Maybe that's the best lesson
anyone learned today."